I have read this book all by myself!

Ahmad G.

_____

(my name)

_____

(date)

US $3.99 / $5.99 CAN

ISBN 0-375-80430-7

50399

9 780375 804304

STEP
into Reading®
A Step 2 Book
Grades 1–3

BATBABY
FINDS A HOME

written and illustrated by
Robert Quackenbush

A NOTE TO PARENTS

When your children are ready to "step into reading," giving them the right books is as crucial as giving them the right food to eat. **Step into Reading Books** present exciting stories and information reinforced with lively, colorful illustrations that make learning to read fun, satisfying, and worthwhile. They are priced so that acquiring an entire library of them is affordable. And they are beginning readers with a difference—-they're written on five levels.

Early Step into Reading Books are designed for brand-new readers, with large type and only one or two lines of very simple text per page. **Step 1 Books** feature the same easy-to-read type as the Early Step into Reading Books, but with more words per page. **Step 2 Books** are both longer and slightly more difficult, while **Step 3 Books** introduce readers to paragraphs and fully developed plot lines. **Step 4 Books** offer exciting nonfiction for the increasingly independent reader.

The grade levels assigned to the five steps—preschool through kindergarten for the Early Books, preschool through grade 1 for Step 1, grades 1 through 3 for Step 2, grades 2 through 3 for Step 3, and grades 2 through 4 for Step 4—are intended only as guides. Some children move through all five steps very rapidly; others climb the steps over a period of several years. Either way, these books will help your child "step into reading" in style!

Ahmad Garcia

To Piet & Margie
—R.Q.

THE OLD BARN

HOUSE WITH CELLAR

CHURCH

NEW HOUSE

SQUIRREL AND WOODPECKER'S HOUSE

FOREST

Copyright © 2001 by Robert Quackenbush. All rights reserved under International and Pan-American Copyright Conventions. Published in the United States by Random House, Inc., New York, and simultaneously in Canada by Random House of Canada Limited, Toronto.
Library of Congress Cataloging-in-Publication Data
Quackenbush, Robert M. Batbaby finds a home / by Robert Quackenbush.
p. cm. — (Step into reading. A step 2 book) Summary: When the barn in which they have been living is knocked down, Batbaby and his parents search for a new home.
ISBN 0-375-80430-7 (trade) — ISBN 0-375-90430-1 (lib. bdg.) [1. Bats—Fiction. 2. Animals—Habitations—Fiction.]
I. Title. II. Step into reading. Step 2 book. PZ7.Q16 Bav 2001 [E]—dc21 00-26410
www.randomhouse.com/kids
Printed in the United States of America July 2001 10 9 8 7 6 5 4 3
STEP INTO READING, RANDOM HOUSE, and the Random House colophon are registered trademarks and the Step into Reading colophon is a trademark of Random House, Inc.

Step into Reading®

BATBABY
FINDS A HOME

Robert Quackenbush

A Step 2 Book

Random House 🏠 New York

Batbaby and his mother and
father lived in an old barn
near the woods.
They were a happy family
of little brown bats.
At night they darted about in
open fields hunting for insects.
During the day they slept
in the cool, dark barn.

One morning Batbaby
couldn't sleep.
He heard strange noises.
"Something bad
is coming," he said.
He woke up
his mother and father.

Batbaby and his mother
and father looked outside.
In the dawn light
they saw a bulldozer.
It came closer
and closer
until...

BOOM! BANG! BAM!

The bulldozer hit the barn!

The barn trembled and shook.

Beams fell and the roof

began to cave in.

Batbaby and his parents

could do only one thing—

fly away.

"We must find a new place

to roost," said Batbaby's father.

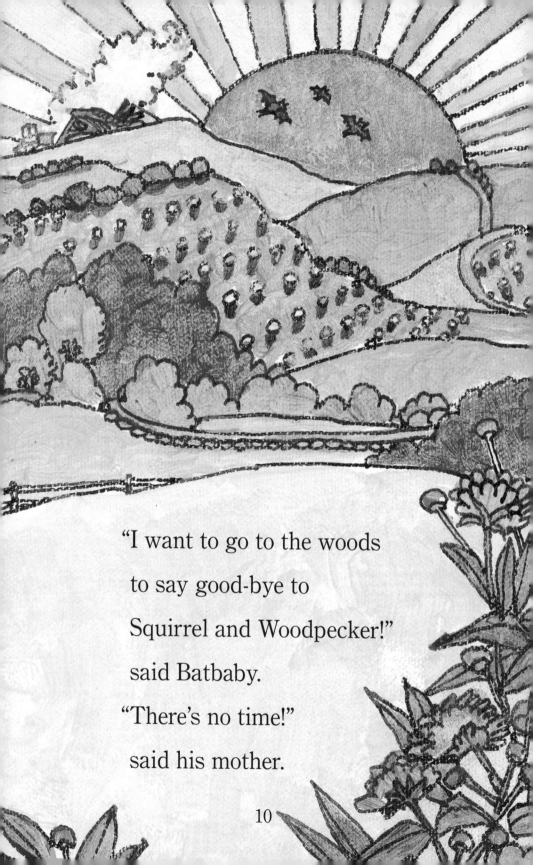

"I want to go to the woods
to say good-bye to
Squirrel and Woodpecker!"
said Batbaby.
"There's no time!"
said his mother.

The bat family flew

as fast as they could

over the countryside.

They came to a little church.

It had a very nice steeple—

just perfect for bats.

11

"Let's stay here,"

said Batbaby's mother.

They flew into the steeple.

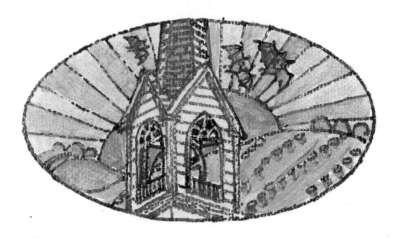

They were very tired.

They folded their wings

and fell sound asleep.

They didn't wake up

until sunset.

"This is a perfect home,"

said Batbaby's father.

But all at once...

BONG! BONG! BONG!

BONG! BONG! BONG!

went the steeple bell.

The loud clanging of the

bell sent the bat family

flying from the steeple.

They were in search

of a new home again.

They flew and flew until
they came to a farmhouse.

They saw an open cellar
window and went inside.
"How dark and cool it is!"
said Batbaby.
"Perfect!" said his mother.
"Dandy!" said his father.
Then they heard...

MEOW! HISS! HISS!

A cat was ready to pounce!

Batbaby and his mother and

father were very scared.

They flew out of the cellar.

They flew and flew until

they came to a tunnel in a hill.

"Perfect," said Batbaby's father.

"But let's eat before we get settled."

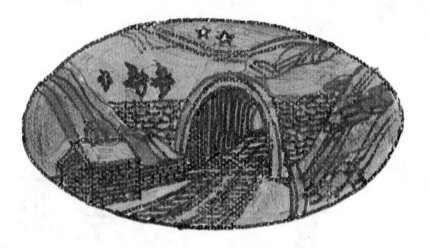

They went to a nearby field.

They gobbled down hundreds

of pesky insects that ruin crops.

Then they flew back to the tunnel.

"How peaceful it is here,"

said Batbaby's mother.

But suddenly…

CHUG! CHUG! CHUG!

HONK! HONK! HONK!

A train came roaring

through the tunnel!

23

Batbaby and his parents
pressed against the ceiling.
They were covered with soot
as the train whizzed past.
Then it was gone.

"Goodness!" said Batbaby's mother.

"What was that?"

"I don't know," said his father.

"But we had better leave

before another one comes along."

Off they flew again.
They flew and flew
until they saw
an old wooden house.

"Old houses have attics,"
said Batbaby's mother.
"We could live there."
But as they went into the
attic, they heard...

HOOT! HOOT!

It was an owl!

"Oh, no," said Batbaby.

"This house is already taken!"

Off they flew again.

They flew from the old house
to a super-highway nearby.
They settled on a steel beam
underneath the highway.
"Perfect!" said Batbaby's father.
But then they heard...

RUMBLE! RUMBLE! RUMBLE!
Cars and trucks on the move
made a lot of noise above them.

"This will never do,"

said Batbaby's mother.

So they flew away, again.

The bat family flew and flew
until they found a tall water tower.
Wind blew and blew around it.
Would the bat family ever
find a nice home?

"I'll ask Squirrel
and Woodpecker
to help us," said Batbaby.
"Be back by sunup,"
said his parents.

Batbaby flew all the way

to where the old barn had been.

Then he flew into the woods.

He flew to the hollow tree where

Squirrel and Woodpecker lived.

Batbaby woke them up.

He told them his problem.

"I know just the place!"

said Squirrel.

"I'll take you there."

They all went

to the far side of the woods.

There was a new house

with a big, beautiful garden!

"But where can my family live?"

Batbaby asked.

Woodpecker pointed.

Batbaby looked.

What did he see?

Fastened to the big house

was a tiny house—just for bats!

"The folks in the new house

want bats to come and protect

their garden from insects,"

said Woodpecker.

In a flash, Batbaby raced back

to the water tower.

Batbaby brought his parents
to see the bat house.
"Just the place!" said his father.

They were settled in
their new home by sunrise.
Thanks to Batbaby, his family's
long night of searching
for a home was over...

. . . and it was truly perfect!

THE TRUTH ABOUT BATS

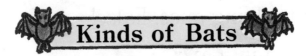

Kinds of Bats

All bats fit into two groups.

The first group is called *Megachiroptera*

(meg-uh-kye-ROP-tur-uh), or "big bats."

They live in the tropics and eat fruit.

The second group is called *Microchiroptera*

(mye-kro-kye-ROP-tur-uh), or "small bats."

Brown bats belong to this group.

Very few bats (1 percent)

are thought of as "vampire bats."

These live mostly in Latin America.

They feed off the blood of cows,

drinking just a few drops at a time

when the cows are asleep.

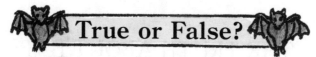
True or False?

Bats get in your hair. False!

Bats are flying mice. False!

Bats are blind. False!

How Bats "See" in the Dark

Bats "see" with "bat sonar"

when they hunt for insects at night.

Bats send out high-pitched sounds.

The sounds bounce off things and

send back echoes that the bats can hear.

A bat can tell by an echo how far away

something is and how big it is.

Using sonar, a brown bat can catch

more than 600 mosquitoes in an hour!

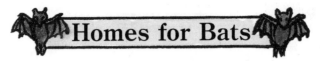

Homes for Bats

The best homes for brown bats

are abandoned mines and bat houses.

Abandoned mines may have metal gates

with small openings.

Bats can get through the gates,

but people can't.

A bat house like the one in this book

can give shelter to a whole group—

or colony—of brown bats.

A bat house has thick walls

to protect bats from the cold.

Inside, the walls should be rough

so bats can cling to them and roost.

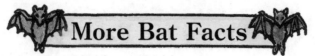

Bats are mammals, like humans

and all other animals

who give milk to their young.

Of all the mammal species in our world,

almost a quarter of them are bats.

Bats are the only mammals that can fly.

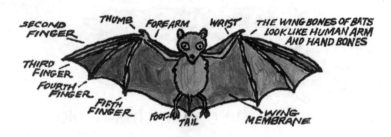

SECOND FINGER THUMB FOREARM WRIST THE WING BONES OF BATS LOOK LIKE HUMAN ARM AND HAND BONES THIRD FINGER FOURTH FINGER FIFTH FINGER FOOT TAIL WING MEMBRANE

They eat pesky bugs, help flowers grow,

and spread the seeds of rain forests.

When bees go to bed, bats go to work.

Bats want to be left alone.

They should never be touched

or bothered in any way.

48